Thanks, Mum

Also by Peter Strawhan and published by Ginninderra Press

Palace of Dreams

Peter Strawhan

Thanks, Mum

Acknowledgements

Huge thanks go to Jane Taylor Robinson, my ever supportive wife – I sure got it right the fourth time, my love! Thanks also to Roger Rees in particular for persuading me that I'm both a poet and a writer and our fellow Sandwriters for their encouragement. Special thanks to Stephen Matthews, who is Ginninderra Press, for starting the ball rolling by publishing my first book of poetry, *Palace of Dreams*.

Thanks, Mum
ISBN 978 1 76041 054 4
Copyright © Peter Strawhan 2015

First published 2015 by
GINNINDERRA PRESS
PO Box 3461 Port Adelaide 5015
www.ginninderrapress.com.au

Contents

Coffee, Anyone?

I fronted up brightly enough to the dull-looking serving woman behind the counter, who reached for her pad and pencil.

'I'm owed one coffee. Make it a flat white, please, and I'll pay for another chai skinny latte.'

Oh dear! All this was a bit too much.

'You what?' she said.

I carefully repeated what I had imagined to be a simple request. But no, I resisted the temptation to use my few words of Italian, or even Greek.

I began again, fairly patiently, as one does with a small child, not one's own. 'The two women at the table by the doorway,' I pointed, 'ordered and paid for three lunches and three coffees, but as I was yet to join them, they asked for my coffee to be held until I arrived. I have now arrived and eaten my lunch and would now like my already paid-for coffee. I wish also to pay for another chai skinny latte for my wife, capisco?'

Non! The large, already red-faced barista man had half-started towards us, but instead called out loudly, 'There was only two coffees on that order slip – a long black and a chai skinny latte.'

The dull one looked disdainfully down her nose at me. My previously bright mood was quickly fading. This is how international incidents and border wars begin, I thought, over storms in coffee cups. I restrained the urge to stamp my foot and swear. Instead, a trifle louder, I again launched into my explanation of what I had thought to be a comparatively simple commercial transaction, but one that was rapidly escalating into a matter of great complexity. Sadly, no magic light appeared in the dull eyes opposing me and the barista man grew even redder.

Just then fate, in the guise of a small kitchen drudge who had overheard our increasingly louder exchanges, intervened. 'It's all right,' she said. 'I took the order while you two were serving tables – it's on the docket.

Oh, the relief as sanity prevailed and order was restored from chaos. I paid for the chai skinny latte and made my way back to our table. The barista man duly served our drinks in silence. In vain, I tried to kill the one fly trying to make my day.

The Never-ending Story

Flo, my ninety-two-year-old widowed mother, has a new ECH support coordinator and one of her three carers reported that she had nothing in her fridge and no food for the weekend. Oh, my God! Little do they realise that Flo won't let them buy her anything. In addition, the poor old thing managed to spill a cup of tea over her lap a week or so back and sustained a nasty burn to her right thigh.

Mum finally phoned me herself. 'The girl kept saying she couldn't connect me, but didn't say why.'

Nothing new here. She'd either scrambled my wife Jane's mobile number or managed to put an extra eight in front of ours.

Her crappy little toaster oven cried enough at about the same time, and brother-in-law John (the supplier) was informed of both calamities, but he and my dear sister, the 'dynamic duo', had been conspicuously absent for some time. 'It's been too hot to go out.' Poor loves. Saddling up the white charger, er, green Honda, we hastened to the rescue yet again and thundered up to Lockleys with our spare mini-oven.

I knocked on the front door while cradling the oven. No response. So we knocked once again and then again. Well, it was ten past eight on a Saturday night. However, there was a light on in the kitchen. Perhaps she's lying on the bathroom floor? Circling the flat, we knocked on the backdoor several times, still no response. But suddenly there was movement in the camp! Shit! There stood Flo in her tatty nightie. Hogarth would have been delighted.

'Did you just knock on the front door? I opened it and there was nobody there!'

Ah! Yes, well.

'Let me put this in the kitchen.'

'How did you know what was wrong with that one?'

'I'm psychic.' (No, I didn't actually say that).

'Well, it's not working, is it?'

Flo thrust a sheaf of papers at me while I was attempting to hook up the new oven. 'Look at these. Why'd they give me all this stuff?'

With great patience I said, warding off the papers, 'I'll look at those in a minute. Now this is how the oven works. OK? Do you understand? That's the oven/grill control, that's the toaster knob. Make sure to switch it off at the wall. You're sure you've got that?'

'Yes.' (And pigs might fly!)

The folder of papers is re-thrust under my nose. 'How do they expect you to read this when it's all done up in plastic?'

'Mum, what you have to do is pull it off like this, then read the contents. Now, here you go, you have them, and you read them. It'll give you something to do.'

(Flo is not impressed.) 'Why didn't you come earlier? You could've had something to eat with me.'

'We couldn't come earlier.'

'Well, you could've come tomorrow, then you could've stayed and had a meal with me.'

'Yes, but we're here now and this is your new oven. You're sure you understand how to work it?'

'If only you'd come earlier, you could've got me some margarine. I haven't got any ice cream either.'

'OK, is there anything else? Milk? I'll see what I can do, back shortly.'

Leaving Jane to face more of the same, I drove off towards town.

Fortunately, the local deli was still open and the friendly Lebanese man remembered me.

Returning to Flo's, I handed over the spoils. 'Here you go – margarine, ice cream, milk.'

'Where'd you get them? You weren't long. How much was it?'

'The deli was still open. That's OK, don't worry about it.'

Flo sat down heavily on a kitchen chair and pulled back the hem of her ancient nightie to reveal a grubby-looking dressing taped over the burn. 'Look at that, the girl came today and changed it. She didn't put the tape on properly, look. How am I expected to keep this on all night?' She peeled back the dressing to reveal ugly red, weeping, scalded flesh.

I had to look away, then forced myself to say, 'Mum, please put the dressing back on and hop into bed. We need to head for home and it's a two-hour drive. We've both had a long day.'

'They sent this big person the other day. He was a man. Funny job for a man to do.'

'Bye, Mum, must go. See you soon.'

'Can't you stay for a cup of tea?'

A week flashed by and no sooner had I arrived at work on Monday morning than the phone rang. I picked it up. 'Strawhan.'

'Is that you, Peter?'

'Yes Mum. How are you?'

'I just rang your number and this other man answered.'

'You must have dialled the wrong number.'

'No I didn't. I'm sure it was the same number.'

'Well, never mind, you've got it right this time. How are you?'

'Lousy, me gums are always sore and I'm sick of eating on me own. Never see a soul unless I go to the club.'

'So you're still managing to get there, that's good. Are you getting a ride, or are you managing to walk?'

'Oh, I've got that trolley thing on wheels I can push and lean on if I get tired. Except on Saturdays, I don't take it then. This woman gives me a ride down, but after the club she goes off to visit her daughter somewhere, so I have to walk home. Anyway, are you all right? John said you've been ill.' (John handles all communication with the world at large; my sister prefers to watch the cricket or tennis while she knits.)

'I've had a bad back, Mum, but it's getting better, just about normal again, thank goodness. When did you see John?'

'No, haven't seen them. Never see anyone. Wouldn't think I had any family. I rang them, thought they might be coming over yesterday, but no. I get sick of sitting here on me own, eating out of a tin.'

'Mum, what do you mean eating out of a tin?'

'Oh, you know, those shiny things the Meals on Wheels leave in the morning. Always too much for me to eat. I just keep putting them in the fridge. Remind me to give you some to take home with you next time you come. Oh! Where was I? Never anyone to talk to and me gums always sore. I asked the girl from the chemists if she could bring me something back. I had a script from the doctor, but it was over thirty dollars so she said she'd cross it out and bring something cheaper. She brought this tube of stuff and it still cost thirteen dollars something. After she went, I found I already had a tube in the cupboard. I'm going to give it back next time she comes.'

'Have you used it on your gums before? Does it help?'

'No, it wasn't for me gums. It was for the other thing.'

'What other thing?'

'Oh, you know. I can't remember what they're called. Anyway, Wendy took me down to that hearing place. I don't know why I bothered. I thought I'd better put those things in me ears. The noise! When I got outside the door, I had to take them out, I couldn't bear the noise.'

'Why didn't you turn them down?'

'Don't know how.'

'But they've got a volume-control. You just need to adjust them.'

'Oh, I don't know. Anyway, he looked in my ears. I forget what he said. I've still got that bill there for thirty-six dollars for those things that go in them. Seems like a waste of money to me.'

'Well, there's not much point paying for new batteries if you're not going to persevere with the hearing aids.'

'Haemorrhoids, that's what the stuff in the tube was for.'

'Jesus wept, Mum!' I exclaimed. 'It's just as well you didn't rub it on your gums, then!'

The Arab

'Do you like junk mail?' the Arab asked seriously.

He does, it seems. It helps him to keep his finger on the pulse of local consumerism. Why, if he didn't read his junk mail religiously, some bargain might escape him.

In the lull before the storm of their departure, he looked over at me. 'What do you usually do Sunday mornings if we're not around?'

'We go to church,' I replied evenly.

His brow puckered. A knowing look spread from ear to ear. 'You're kidding,' he ventured.

I smiled.

The three scrapbooks on the table next took his eye. 'What's this?'

'Motorcycle scrapbooks.'

'Can I have a look?'

I nodded.

'Are they interesting?'

'Only if you like motorcycles, I imagine,' came my smart-arsed reply.

His mother thinks he has a fantastic sense of humour. I think he is a clown. No wonder his second wife eventually departed, following the example of her predecessor.

The Arab is a man of hobbies. He regulates his life by a meticulous division of leisure time. His hobbies are legion. Although he thinks he might abandon the model aeroplanes (including the latest, a radio controlled helicopter), the crossbows, the lepidoptera collection, the square dancing, the badminton, and whatever else one should happen to mention, for a single all-encompassing passion, the restoration of a vintage car.

'Do you have a book on Bugattis?'

Regrettably, I do not.

The Arab thinks he would like one – a Bugatti, that is. 'Not the racing one with the alloy wheels, the one after, the sports car, beautiful!'

Dear God! I control my impatience at the absurdity heaped upon absurdity and steadfastly maintain an aloof silence.

The Arab continues to prattle on whilst idly flicking through the pages of my motorcycle scrapbooks. I wince as the corner of one page tears. He, of course, seems not to notice. Eventually he reaches the end of the last book and leaves the room.

I begin to relax. There is laughter from the passage and the blue shimmer of a camera flash. His mother is taking her son's photograph, a plus for posterity. He is dressed appropriately in a burnous, recently brought back from Egypt by a friend. To my jaundiced eye he still looks like a clown. The Pagliacci of the desert, or an extra escaped from a Crosby and Hope movie. The black moustache drooping lewdly past the corners of his mouth reinforces this impression.

The Arab and his entourage leave soon afterwards.

His latest woman parcels her three compliant children aboard the battered blue Kombi and thanks us for our hospitality. 'See youse all later,' she smiles.

Pulling on his string-backed driving gloves, the Arab climbs into place behind the small, custom-made alloy steering wheel. The Kombi rattles into life, belching blue smoke, and with a protesting shudder from the clutch lurches away up the street. The Arab crouches low over the wheel and manages to clip the kerb with the nearside rear tyre as he accelerates through the slight bend towards the main road. He waves a nonchalant hand to demonstrate his complete control over the machine. He is away in his very own Bugatti. The blue smoke haze slowly dissipates. We are left with his mother and her husband. It is still Sunday.

Le Chat Noir

It all started because she closed the bedroom door but didn't shut it firmly enough to engage the tongue. Not her tongue, of course – that was always engaged. On and on, as if she had discovered a new source of perpetual motion. All that was needed was a bit of pressure, a firm push, or even a turn of the handle with the push. Not difficult. I could always manage, why couldn't she?

Bloody cat landed on the bed in the small hours; it knew the door would yield to a small push. Smart cat. Knowing. Hated my guts. The feeling was mutual. Sounds like an ad for medical benefits, or life assurance.

She pushed the cat away, the black mass, purring in the dark, its claws clutching and releasing in primeval anticipation. Fair enough. Except that it hooked one needle-sharp claw in my shoulder as she connected. The cat landed on the floor with a yowl and a thump. I sat up with a louder yell as its claw tore my flesh. Fucking cat.

Cunning as a shithouse rat, that cat. I got the .22 out one day, after it had crapped in the kitchen once too often. It stared up at me with that unblinking look of disdain, as if its shit didn't stink. When

I cocked the rifle, it took off like a Bondi tram. Must have been three days before it ghosted in one night; I'd cooled down by then. Her cat. Her kitchen. Her cat's shit to clean up. Why should I worry?

I stood over it with a lump of four-by-two once. Saw the bloody thing jump onto the bonnet of my car. My car. Not her car. It knew. A lazy leap in the sun, but didn't quite have the energy, so it slid down the slope of the bonnet with its claws extended. Right through the fucking duco. I swung and missed. Fucking cat, but my turn would come.

We moved again about then, and things seemed to get better, for a while. Then I walked into the kitchen one day, looking for a bite of lunch. There was the bloody cat in mid-stride with a half-thawed salmon trout in its mouth. Just for once, I was too quick for it. My boot connected with its backside with a satisfying thunk. The cat mewed loudly, dropped the fish and disappeared through its escape hatch in the screen door.

All that week, she kept asking me whether I'd seen it. She even went out looking for the bloody useless thing, searched the neighbourhood, calling out its name. The flies had a great time swimming in the saucers of milk she kept putting outside the back door.

Then it was Sunday, our lie-in morning. She lay there, fretting about the cat. I began to wonder whether I'd actually hurt it when my boot connected. Bad luck if I had. The cat's bad luck, not mine. I wasn't superstitious.

I got up eventually and put the kettle on. Then went outside for a leak and there was the poor bloody cat. Just skin and bone with its arse-end dragging on the ground. It was long past running. I went inside and got an old bath towel from the cupboard in the spare room and some mince from the fridge. It followed me around to the back of the shed and I put the dish of mince on the ground in front of its nose. When it started to feed, I grabbed it as gently as I could around the neck with one hand and wrapped it in the towel. It struggled a bit then stopped moving. I grabbed the spade and dug a hole down the back corner, near the apple tree. I carried the small bundle down and laid it in the hole. I thought the towel moved, so I gave it a couple of hard whacks with the spade, then filled the soil back and patted it down.

I went back inside, washed my hands, then boiled the water and made some tea. While the tea was drawing, I switched on the toaster and loaded a tray. 'There you go', I said, 'breakfast in bed. Tell you what, I think that cat of your's a bloody lost cause. Why don't we drive into town tomorrow and get you a nice little kitten?'

Volvo With Black Triangles

We were both members of the same protest group and had a nodding acquaintance. I knew Annie was divorced and spoke of three teenage daughters. I'd been living on my own for the past couple of years and rather fancied the idea of romancing her into my bed, should the opportunity present itself. Typically, I'd spent too much time thinking about the prospect without actively pursuing the quarry at meetings or other social events.

On my way home from visiting an ancient aunt who lived on the west coast, I stopped off in Port Augusta for lunch and a cold beer. Refreshed, I left the shady comfort of the pub's beer garden and wandered back towards the car park, blinking in the harsh sunlight. My sunglasses seemed to have disappeared, then I realised I'd managed to leave them sitting on the table. As I turned hurriedly to retrace my steps, I bumped, full tilt, into another person. We fended each other off in a flurry of hands and arms as we each muttered an automatic apology. Then recognition dawned: it was Annie.

'My God! What are you doing in Port Augusta,' we exclaimed in unison.

Turned out she had joined a group of similarly minded mothers with assorted children, on a weekend trip to the arid lands botanic gardens. They were about to have a picnic lunch at a nearby reserve.

I declined Annie's invitation to join the party, but as we gave each other a rather enjoyable and lingering hug, plucked up the courage to say what I was thinking. 'Um,' I ventured, 'Annie, whenever we bump in to each other, I find myself thinking how much I'd like to…' I paused. 'Yes,' as she continued pressing her pelvis against mine. 'Phew, it's warming up,' I croaked, then plunged on. '…how much I'd like to get you into bed.'

Annie batted her long eyelashes at me. 'I don't see anything wrong with that idea,' she murmured, squeezing my hand.

We hastily exchanged phone numbers, gave each other a final clinch then went our separate ways.

Back home, a week or more faded by as routine inevitably resumed its dominance. I pottered around in my small vegie garden and cut back the odd native that threatened to takeover.

A mate phoned late one night to remind me of the monthly bistro at the local yacht club that I'd agreed to attend. I thanked him for the reminder, but not with a great deal of enthusiasm, given the usual paucity of attractive women.

I poured myself a final nightcap glass of red and found myself thinking of attractive and not-so-attractive women I'd made love to over the years. My love life had been pretty well non-existent since the latest divorce. In fact, I'd begun to think I might never have another relationship, let alone a one-night stand.

Fortunately, before I became completely maudlin, I suddenly remembered my brief encounter with Annie and the promise of a mutually rewarding re-match. I looked at the time and decided, what the hell, it was late, but I doubted she was an early to bed girl. Nonetheless, I paused before pressing the final digit, then the red wine took over and Annie's voice licked my ear.

I heard her old Volvo station wagon pull up out the front of my place on Saturday night, almost on time, just as she'd promised. My spirits lifted in anticipation of what I hoped was to come.

'Come in, come in,' as I opened the front door and we gave each other a quick hug and a peck on the cheek. 'Here you go, nice cold glass of bubbly.'

We clinked glasses and eyed each other over the rims.

'Dinner's just about ready. Hope you like chicken breasts stuffed with camembert, in a cream and white wine sauce?'

'Sounds lovely,' Annie responded. 'I didn't know you were a gourmet cook.'

'Ah, well,' I heard myself simpering, 'let's hope it's edible!'

I'd kept the meal simple, with fruit salad and ice cream to follow the mains. We soon disposed of the champagne and got stuck into one of my good bottles of a local red. Then it was time to move to the lounge for coffee and some quiet mood music from my old stereo system. It was also time to move more intimate matters along. Throughout the meal, while I'd concentrated on performing as the perfect host, Annie had kept prattling about the Coorong and how much she enjoyed spending time there alone, exploring all the wilderness had to offer.

With coffee out of the way, we'd gravitated into each other's arms on the smaller lounge and our lips sought and found their respective targets. As we both settled in to enjoying our initial exploration of mouths, ears, necks, I couldn't believe the ease of my good fortune. It seemed as if my personal drought was about to be well and truly broken.

Taking the initiative, or rather Annie's hands, I led her at length into my darkened bedroom, but left the door to the lounge open so the light shone through onto the king-sized bed. She offered no resistance as I guided her down on top of the duvet, but lazily stretched out with a contented sigh. I hastily shed my slacks, jocks and shirt. Neither of us had bothered with shoes.

I slid my now sweaty fingers along the waistband of her tight black jeans, slipping undone the top button, then, full of anticipation, eased down the zip. Annie lifted her deliciously small backside without a murmur as I pulled the jeans gently away from those long, tanned legs and tossed them to one side. She had a wonderful body under the black T-shirt and I couldn't see any stretch marks. Her full breasts were without a bra and her nipples stood firm and large. As I peeled down her black briefs, another, oh so black triangle appeared. I kneeled at her feet and drank her in, but my loins did not stir as she lay there motionless beneath my gaze.

'Please don't make me pregnant,' Annie whispered.

'No fear of that,' I responded, caressing the smoothness of those enticing breasts in one last futile attempt to restore my lost libido, knowing full well she was already lost to me. Her focus was the Coorong, to where she had already flown.

My apology was brief and we dressed in silence. I stood at the front door until the Volvo started up and its headlights lit the dark street.

I wandered back inside and slumped down in the lounge with the last of the red Annie had left in her glass. Typically, my wits had deserted me. Why hadn't I flown away with her to the Coorong. We could have made love among the dunes, heard the lap of waves under the watchful moon. Instead, another small death blow to my already fragile reputation as the great Lothario.

Then the phone rang. My first thought, it's Annie, the Volvo's broken down. My pulse quickened.

Wrong, it was Rob at the yacht club bistro. 'Mate, where the fuck are you? Get over here pronto. I've got this red-headed bird wants to meet you.

After the Funeral

We arrived as instructed, on the hour, to collect Florence from her neat, cream-brick unit in the tight cluster of clones that held more of her kind set around the courtyard with its contoured bark-chip-covered burial-like mounds. The blank windows were mute witness to our arrival, although I fancy a curtain moved. My sister and her husband stayed with his precious red Magna, the threat of theft always heavy on their minds. I knocked carefully on the front security door to avoid damage to my knuckles.

At my mother's querulous enquiry, I announced myself, turned my key in the lock and stepped into the habitual gloom of her small front room. She was already dressed impeccably in her favourite lemon suit, hair freshly coloured and permed. In the subdued light she favoured, sitting on the floral lounge with the crossword open on her lap, she looked remarkably well preserved for a woman in her late eighties. I stooped and gave her the obligatory peck on the cheek, which was about as much physical contact as there had ever been between us. I just managed to avoid losing my left eye on the frame of her glasses as she turned her head.

Her concern, of course, was not with the fact of her younger brother's funeral; rather it was the weather that seriously engaged her attention. What was it like out? Would she be too hot? She had already changed her outfit once, it transpired. However was I supposed to know the precise temperature which would satisfy her needs? I said nothing. To be charitable, perhaps it was her only way of coping with the fact of her sibling's demise? Clearly, I will never know.

As always, she then began her standard litany of trivia. The armour of minutiae automatically assembled to protect her against the reality of her existence. I had already been subjected to this per my daily telephone call, so I tried to combat her negativity with some positive thoughts of my own. It was to no avail. In desperation, I managed to break the flow by pointing to the clock on the mantelpiece and exclaiming that it was time we left for the funeral parlour. I shepherded her out to the Magna, waiting in the bright glare of summer sunlight, hastily donning my dark glasses in the process.

I opened the left-hand rear door and stood patiently as my mother lowered herself gingerly into place, complaining all the while about the difficulty of the operation, her sore knees and the cramped confines of my brother-in-law's pride and joy.

Without turning her head, my sister commanded, as one would a child, 'Mother, please put your seat belt on.'

I hastily moved around to the other side, buckled myself into place, then leaned across and secured mother's belt.

My brother-in-law carefully inspected us both in the rear-vision mirror, selected reverse gear with grave deliberation, and backed out into the driveway. There was a sudden screech of brakes and the blast of a car horn from behind us. The Magna rocked as my brother-in-law applied the brakes and a huge four-wheel drive accelerated past with a derisory blast from its air horns. A large red-faced man in the driver's seat waved his fist.

My mother waved a gloved hand in a queenly gesture towards the tiny, silver-haired woman looking distraught at his side. 'Just what I'd expect from that ignorant lout,' she sniffed. They've only been in that unit Brenda used to have for five minutes. Don't know why she had to die when she did. She wasn't even my age.'

My sister sighed loudly.

We cruised slowly down the access driveway, passing the serried ranks of wheelie bins leaning against the brush fences which cloistered the rotary clotheslines from inquisitive eyes. Joining the main road maclstrom, we headed sedately towards the highway, travelling in mutual silence, save for the audible and incessant grinding of Florence's lower jaw. This was an annoying and now reflex habit she had recently acquired.

The car park at the rear of the funeral parlour already held a sprinkling of early arrivals. As we pulled in to an empty slot, a large Ford sailed past and dipped sloppily to a halt, disgorging a seemingly endless cargo of chattering young people. They appeared to be dressed for a night at the theatre. It occurred to me that in a way it could be seen as such, or rather a morning performance, in a minor key. You will notice, to my credit, that I avoided the pun. This was now the final rite of passage, in which we all had our small set pieces to play. My mother raised an eyebrow but, on this occasion at least, said nothing.

The feeling of theatre continued inside the building. Initially it was much cooler, but as the number of mourners grew, the discrete air-conditioning failed to cope adequately. One hoped that the refrigeration plant concealed somewhere behind all the gold and pastel decor was up to its task. My sister, her husband, and I, found seats near the back. Florence's only surviving brother, with the help of his wife, who was a good deal younger than either of them, guided her to the front stalls. There was a hush of expectation.

The funeral director was tall and rotund, a living advertisement for his craft. He wore a sober, charcoal grey double-breasted suit; there was a white carnation in his lapel. He was perspiring freely and, Pavarotti-like, frequently mopped the sheen from his temple with what appeared to be a large white table napkin. His slight gesture must have activated a remote sensor, for an unseen choir began to sing while simultaneously the drapes at the end of the room parted silently. He beamed benignly over us his captive audience, as the house lights dimmed and a battery of spotlights lit up the honey-coloured coffin, now revealed in its lonely alcove at centre stage. A large sheaf of red roses, probably from my uncle's garden, nestled consolingly on its lid together with a pair of chrome-plated secateurs.

The clergyman, who now made his entrance from stage right, was from a similar genetic production line to the director. Fittingly, however, he was clad in a designer version of a monkish white robe. Sadly, this just failed to conceal the lower section of his trouser-suited legs. The wardrobe department had also erred in the matter of footwear: instead of leather sandals, his large feet were encased in black nylon socks and brown brogues. Happily, he was possessed of a most mellifluous bass voice.

The eulogy was as comprehensive as any that I have heard and documented in great detail the many aspects of my late uncle's long life, including his love of gardening, his sporting prowess as a young man and a good deal more. The recently departed, he assured us, with the unctuous ease of a seasoned performer, had merely slipped away into another room. We could rest comfortably in the certain knowledge that our dear friend, and/or relative, was simply waiting for us, just around the corner. This was a message that I found a touch disconcerting, to say the least. We were invited to pray. A glance around me at the still faces and bowed heads suggested that I was, perhaps, alone with my concern.

As we joined together in a rather ragged rendition of 'Amazing Grace', the immediate family, including Florence, were invited to view the deceased for one last time. The curtains closed behind them, thus concealing this arcane segment of the ritual, and we sat in silence for what seemed a very long few minutes. For some unaccountable reason, this interval rather reminded me of that part of the marriage service when the chief participants disappear to sign their relationship into law. The chief mourners eventually reappeared through a side door, leaving my uncle to his well-earned peace. Strangers would soon accompany him on his final drive.

The lights sprang up and lissom young hostesses moved smilingly amongst us, dispensing welcome cups of tea and coffee. There had also appeared plates of assorted sweet biscuits on small tables, tucked discreetly to one side. The buzz of conversation became louder, as friends and relatives who had not met since the last such occasion caught up with the events of the intervening years.

Florence was in her element. She had taken up a strategic position in one of the few large, leather-covered lounge chairs and was holding court to a small but select number of cronies and acolytes. As was always the case in such circumstances, the volume of her voice rose along with the pitch. My sister and her husband hovered anxiously nearby, keeping a watchful eye on Florence while exchanging matters of note with various cousins, both near and removed.

I took the opportunity to approach my newly widowed aunt, a diminutive woman in her late seventies, who still retained her girlish zest for life.

We gave each other a hug and she kissed me full on the lips. 'There's one for my favourite nephew,' she whispered in my ear. Hope 'Flo's watching. Do her good.'

Her breath smelt richly of brandy and I found myself thinking longingly of a large measure, with ice and soda. It was clear that she was bearing up well under the strain of her loss.

I knew how much she and my uncle had meant to each other and I had always admired them both. They were one of the few married couples I could bring to mind who, after a lifetime together, were still patently in love. In fact, most of the more recently married of my acquaintance were already aground on the rocks of marital discord. My late father, I am sure, was now resting easily, having finally escaped from my dear mother's withering grasp. Wedded bliss, it seemed to me, was, generally speaking, something of an oxymoron.

Across the now diminished throng, Florence called out to me sharply, breaking in to my comfortable musing. 'Where is your sister? It's time we were going.' Evidently she had exhausted herself, or her audience; besides which it was well past her usual midday lunchtime.

We said our farewells, which involved me in another kiss and hug from my aunt, who by now was becoming a little teary-eyed. Mother was not amused at this flagrant display of affection and hissed at me to wipe the vivid red smear of lipstick from my mouth.

She stumbled on the steps leading down to the car park, but testily shook off my proffered arm. My brother-in-law helped her into the Magna and she pointedly ignored my attempt at conversation as we drove down the highway. Instead, she addressed herself to my sister, who sat silently, staring blankly at the glowing stop lights of the car in front.

'I do think the minister went on about Gordon for far too long, don't you?' she enquired.

My sister maintained her silence. It occurred to me that this was Florence's only comment to date about her younger brother's demise.

'Answer me! All that boring prattle! Who could possibly be interested in how many jobs he had and what he did in the war? Answer me! I'm talking to you, my girl!' Her voice rose as she reached forward and prodded my sister in the ribs.

'Mother, will you please fasten your seat belt,' was the icily delivered rejoinder, as she twisted out of range.

That exchange exhausted the conversation until we reached the unit.

'Oh! I didn't realise you were driving me straight home. I thought we would go back to your place for a bite of lunch together,' Florence said, almost plaintively.

'No mother, not today,' from my sister.

'But I haven't had a meal with you for so long.'

'I'm sorry, Mother. I've had enough for one day. I simply cannot handle funerals.'

I rather hoped that mother did not hear the quietly spoken 'or you', that my sister added. Mind you, if it had been anyone else, I would have expected something even stronger, but my sister had never approved of swearing and I doubted she knew a single four-letter word. I then remembered that as children we had always been spared attendance at the funerals of various relatives, even my mother's parents. We were told after the event, a protective practice that had continued until we became of age.

I led the way inside, with my sister reluctantly bringing up the rear. My brother-in-law was attempting to mollify Florence over the matter of lunch, but by now she had decided that we should stay and eat with her.

She seized upon me as her most likely ally. 'Come on,' she said, 'you must be starving. There's a cold chicken in the fridge and we can soon make a salad.' She noted my hesitation. 'Or what about a nice chicken sandwich?'

I wavered. 'Well, it has been rather a long morning.'

'No, Mother,' my sister interjected. 'We really are going. We have to feed the dog.'

She ushered my brother-in-law towards the door. He looked at me and gave a slight shrug, then followed her out.

I tried to pat my mother reassuringly on the arm, but she was now in her frustrated little girl mode and refused to be placated. I mumbled an apology. I was a passenger only and had no choice but to leave with my sister and her husband. I would telephone in the morning, as usual.

The three of us made our way out to the Magna. My brother-in-law started the motor. As he did so, my mother appeared like an avenging fury.

She hurled the cold chicken in its plastic shroud through the open window onto my sister's ample lap and screamed at the top of her lungs, 'If you refuse to eat here with me, you might as well take the chicken home with you.' She turned awkwardly on her unsteady heel and rushed back inside.

My sister had reared up in her seat with a cry of anguish as the cold chicken landed between her legs then thumped on the rubber mat. It was a rather large bird.

With great presence of mind, my brother-in-law manoeuvred the Magna towards the road.

'Stop the car', my sister shrieked.

He hurriedly complied and turned to look at her. 'What now, my dear?' he enquired soothingly.

'Just this,' my sister replied very quietly. 'AAAAAHHHH! The bitch, the bloody fucking old bitch,' she yelled, for the entire world to hear.

I was quite taken aback; I had never heard my sister swear before.

Brompton

My earliest recollections are merely a faded collection of snapshots. A birthday gift, a silk-covered, wire-framed model aeroplane, with a wooden propeller driven by winding up a rubber band. I doubt it survived for long. This was at Brompton in about 1936 and I was four years old. A Saturday night treat, chocolate-coated clinkers from the shop at the corner, somehow associated with the smell of pea soup. My younger sister and I dressed up as bride and groom in home-made formal wedding clothes for a fancy dress contest at the Hindmarsh Town Hall. We may even have won a prize. More strongly, I recall waking in the cold of many mornings with my eyes gummed shut by a yellow discharge and the sting of hard soap when my mother washed the lids open.

Home was one of a row of attached workmen's cottages in East Street, almost in the shadow of the giant gasometer that dominated the skyline. The stench from the gasworks was all-pervading. My maternal grandparents lived nearby in Chief Street. They had managed to rear their brood of seven children in a tiny cottage which boasted two underground bedrooms. Next door lived their youngest daughter, my Auntie Ethel, with her husband and, eventually, ten of my cousins. At the rear, behind a low stone wall, lay a former pug hole, now a rubbish dump. This was our playground and a constant source of delight as we unearthed fascinating items to include in our games. Copper, brass and other non-ferrous metals were added to Grandfather's collection, for later sale to the scrap metal dealer. Across the road was a tannery, which offered some competition to the gasworks in generating the always-present noxious odours.

My grandfather had a small, untidy workshop with a large, hand-driven grindstone standing sentinel at the doorway. All sorts of arcane tools lay on the battered wooden bench and lurked in every dark corner, most veiled in the webs of spiders, either living or long dead. The rough timbered floor was layered in sawdust and wood shavings and I remember savouring the full-bodied smell of linseed oil. Grandpa Mac was a fierce little man, with a Neville Chamberlain-like moustache hiding a weak mouth. He always seemed to wear a waistcoat over his work shirt and navy trousers, with a pair of bike clips permanently sited above battered old boots to complete the ensemble.

His voice croaked asthmatically, a probable legacy of the years he'd spent labouring in the nearby brickyards, then later, breathing in coal dust for the rest of his working life. Eventually, like many other South Australians of the inter-war years, he'd managed to get a job on the railways. Until his retirement, Grandpa Mac worked as a wheel checker; this entailed walking along beside trains in the railway yards and tapping each of the cast-iron wheels with a special hammer. A cracked wheel gave off a different sound to a solid wheel. This tedious and potentially dangerous job had to be carried out in daylight or darkness and in all weathers. Not an enviable occupation.

My grandmother was larger and rounder. She gave a superficial appearance of warmth and jollity, but behind her small, round glasses the eyes were cold and unfriendly; perhaps she had had enough of little boys. Three strong memories remain. The look and feel of the wooden handled knives and forks in her kitchen, which lived in a small drawer built into the side of the oilcloth-covered wooden table. Then there was the delight of hanging cherries over my ears, around that same table one Christmas with my sister and cousins all crowded together, and then tasting the sweetness of the ripe fruit.

On what I still remember as a rather less pleasant occasion, I was lying on the threadbare and dusty carpet in the front room, glancing through a picture book that the cousins had discarded. Grandma was sitting in her favourite chair making the latest in a legion of now politically incorrect black golliwogs, when my sister wandered in and snatched the book from my hands. I rose in protest momentarily then, as usual, gave in to her demand and subsided onto my back. Without thinking, I arched my back, lifted my legs up and began cycling in the air. As I completed each revolution, my hips in turn gave a discernible 'clunk'.

Grandma Mac peered through her black-framed glasses at me and spoke for the first time since I'd entered her domain. 'You'll have rheumatism when you get older,' she declaimed, 'mark my words.'

I have done so over these many years.

Full Circuit

Diminished by age and illness, he was standing alone in the gloomy corridor when we arrived. His arms at his side were bent forward, as if he was tentatively reaching for someone or something. He was groaning, quite loudly, 'If I had a gun, I'd know what to do. If I had a gun, I'd know what to do.' Over and over, like a mantra he'd just invented. When he saw her, his face lit up, the groaning stopped. As we approached, he moved to take her hands and tried to kiss her. She avoided his clumsy embrace and averted her face to avoid his tremulous lips. Her distaste was evident. A due reward, for daring to succumb to his illness and thereby disturbing her pattern of existence after all the long decades of their marriage.

He registered my presence for the first time and held out his right hand. We shook hands briefly. His grip was surprisingly firm and his skin was warm to the touch. Taking his arm, I led him off along the corridor towards the day room.

He suddenly came to a halt. 'What's your name?' he asked.

I told him.

'I'm George,' he said.

We solemnly shook hands again.

Thelma had disappeared, no doubt to swoop on one of the more congenial women of her acquaintance. Probably the one who had refused to believe her age on a previous visit; Thelma had, of course, preened.

Meanwhile, George had begun groaning again.

I patted his arm as one might pat a child on the head. 'It's all right, George, take it easy,' I said. 'What's the problem?'

'The blood, the blood. I had blood all over me, down here.' He indicated his dark blue tracksuit pants, which showed evidence of nothing more sinister than a few food stains.

'You're OK now, 'I hastened to reassure him. 'All cleaned up.'

I manoeuvred him over to one of the large reclining armchairs facing the western windows and gently helped him to arrange himself in its depths. He farted loudly, but the other patients, all in varying stages of decay, were safely cocooned in their own fantasy worlds and oblivious to such minor occurrences. One or two were sitting directly in front of the enormous television set which dominated the far corner of the room. If the jangling outpouring of messages to buy and consume were registering on its captive viewers, their impassive faces gave nothing away. In counterpoint, at the other end of the room was an equally enormous and gaudily hued Coke machine. I was mildly surprised that nobody was eyeing their own reflection in its vast, shiny surface.

Meanwhile, Thelma had reappeared, offering no explanation for her absence. George had dozed off but she shook him awake with her hand on his arm. He looked dazed, and uncomprehending.

'Where's your good pullover, George?' she demanded. 'Why are you wearing that awful cardigan, for goodness sake? That's not yours. And just look at those pants: they're only fit for the ragbag. They're not your slippers either. What's happened to your good slippers?'

With each question, her voice became louder and more strident. I winced. His face quivered and his hands went over his ears. A tear formed in the corner of his right eye. I watched it negotiate the hollow of his cheek and disappear in the stubble under his jawline.

At that point, the duty sister appeared, wheeling a small, white-painted trolley. 'Medicine time, Georgy,' she decreed cheerfully. 'Sit up like a good boy.' She handed him several pills in a throwaway plastic cup.

George dutifully helped himself to the pills, as if they were so many boiled sweets. He grimaced each time he awkwardly washed down a pill with a sip of water from the glass she proffered in her other hand.

'That's the way, well done!' She turned to Thelma, who hastily came to attention. 'Poor old boy had a bit of an accident this morning. We didn't quite make it to the toilet in time. That's why he's wearing those old tracksuit pants and the cardigan. His own stuff's a bit of a mess, I'm afraid. We had to chuck his slippers in the bin. They just fell apart when we hosed him down. No good buying those proper carpet slippers. Vinyl's the only thing we get any mileage out of in here. Funny thing is, he thought he was bleeding. The mind does strange things. I guess he would've preferred blood to shit, eh, Georgy?' She laughed.

Thelma looked down her nose but remained silent for once.

The sister continued, 'Actually, he's been making a bit of a nuisance of himself since you were here last. Frightening some of our old ladies. Wandering into their rooms during the night. He's lonely, just trying to be friendly, but we might have to move him to the restricted access section soon. Bit sad, really, but we have to think of the others. Somebody might think he was up to no good, mightn't they, Georgy?' She winked at me and laughed again.

I resisted the impulse to tell her to shut up and hated myself for smiling instead.

Thelma sniffed, as if to say, 'I might have known. He's not to be trusted, never been any different as long as I've known him.' Then she smiled sweetly, 'Whatever you think's best, dear. I don't envy you your job at all.'

Sister nodded in agreement and resumed her pill-dispensing round.

George was slumped back in the depths of the chair. Over the months of his confinement, his skin had yellowed like parchment, while his nose had become more prominent. There was a deep imprint in the bridge where his heavy glasses usually sat. He was no longer wearing them, or his dentures. Without his teeth, the lower part of his face seemed to have caved in, along predetermined fault lines. There was an angry shaving rash around his neck; it was spotted with dried blood and small patches of hair missed by the nurse's razor. He began groaning again, more quietly this time.

Thelma reached over and patted him on the arm. 'That's enough of that,' she hissed. 'Stop making a nuisance of yourself.'

George looked at her with expressionless eyes. I noticed the white circles around his irises. I remembered somebody telling me years ago that they were a sure indication of imminent death. I hastily looked away. He attempted to stand up, but when his body had trouble obeying he became agitated.

It was my turn to pat his arm. 'It's OK, George. Take it easy.'

He subsided, but began kicking the leg of Thelma's chair with his slippered right foot, like a petulant child.

Thelma resumed her questioning. 'What did you have for lunch, George? He must know what he had for lunch,' she appealed to me.

I shrugged; it was patently obvious to me that his condition had deteriorated markedly since our previous visit. She seemed unwilling, or unable, to grasp the reality of his decline. Perhaps to do so would be an admission of Thelma's own mortality. It could also be an indication of her complete preoccupation with her own well-being.

I decided to create a diversion. 'Cup of tea, George?' I enquired.

He continued to focus on his right foot as it swung back and forth, tapping away against Thelma's chair.

'I'll have one, thanks,' she said, her lips set in their customary downward line.

I rinsed out three thick-rimmed cups in the adjacent kitchen and wiped them with a tea towel that had seen better days. There were saucers on the shelf and I found tea bags in an old coffee tin. I ignored the notice commanding visitors to place twenty cents in the receptacle provided. Another tin contained a few slightly soft biscuits and there was milk in the fridge. The instant hot water was almost boiling.

I commandeered one of the small tables, slewed it around in front of George and Thelma, then handed them their tea. George needed both of his trembling hands to convey the cup to his mouth. Thelma turned her nose up at the biscuits, but still managed to eat a couple in quick succession. George set his cup back on its saucer with some difficulty and used the same two-handed technique to cram most of a biscuit between his lips. He was less successful with his cup handling at the next attempt and managed to spill tea down the front of his ancient cardigan. He looked down at the rivulet of tea and biscuit crumbs and then at Thelma, with what almost amounted to the beginning of a smile.

Before she could launch into the attack, I grabbed a length of paper towel from the dispenser in the kitchen and mopped him down. 'Come along, old chap,' I said, helping him to his feet, 'let's have a look at the garden.'

It was warmer out of doors and we both blinked in the sudden glare of what should have been a wintry sun. Beneath my fingers his arm felt thin and fragile. We made our way slowly along the path, which looped between manicured beds of roses and then a more casual collection of native trees and shrubs.

George, unlike his wife, had always been a gardener. He'd once grown roses, dahlias and carnations in profusion and, of course, gladioli, now that ultimate symbol of the suburbia in which he had largely spent his days. It was clear that the flowers and shrubs no longer held meaning for him. His life had dwindled down to a few primary sensations, heat and cold, hunger and thirst, pain and the absence of pain; not much else remained.

The sun disappeared behind the clouds and he shivered. We completed our circuit and returned to the side entrance of the building.

In the doorway stood Thelma, tongue poised.

'Are you ready to go, Mother?' I asked, before she could speak. 'I'll just take Dad back to his room.'

Kevin

If 'crepuscular' meant what it sounds as if it should mean, then it would have described Kevin to a tee. He was revolting. His pale skin erupted in ugly, yellow pus-oozing sores. His lank hair was Brylcreemed flat. He was round-shouldered and flat-footed, and his incipient pot belly thrust forward in the tight-banded but wide-bottomed flairs. He wore black winkle-picker shoes, with square buckles and odd socks which were impressively holed. His once-white nylon shirt gaped open over the pot belly, where a button or two had gone missing. A broad, floral tie hung awkwardly, thanks to its perished elastic neckband.

In short, Kevin was a creep. He sidled up to unwary strangers at parties and lisped into his introductory line. 'Hello, I'm Kevin. What's your name?' That was enough to send people scattering for miles. If they were foolish enough, or stoned enough to stand their ground, the next words to issue from between his yellowed teeth – which were enhanced by the occasional black hole – finished the rout. 'You look nice,' and Kevin was alone.

It was sad, really. I mean, the poor bastard couldn't help it. Or could he? Anyway, it was more or less OK until Kevin homed in on

Viv. She was in a fair old state at the time, as I'd all ready discovered. I was in some mild marital strife myself. 'So what's new?' did I hear you say? Fair enough. Viv had just told Syd that she'd been having it off with young Marcus. Syd couldn't handle the news and screamed off in their beat-up old Datsun as if it was a Porsche turbo.

We exchanged commiserations about men who couldn't or wouldn't understand how they weren't the be all and end all of our existence.

As Viv said, she wanted room to move. It was her body and if she wanted a little variation, that was her business. Mind you, the way that Marcus is built I don't know about 'little' variation! Anyway, if Syd couldn't handle the situation that was a pity, but it wouldn't have broken her up if he'd wanted the odd stray encounter. What was wrong with the over-possessive bastard anyway? The more she talked about it, the more pissed off she became. The booze helped. Well, a bit too much, actually. I mean, I didn't really intend to let it slip about me and Marcus. It just kind of came out. Fucking Kevin and that bag of dope. Mind you, I still don't know how Viv could bring herself to do it. Fancy her pissing off into the twilight with the creepy little bastard in his BMW.

A Mini-affair

We were lingering over our coffee, chatting quietly about bikes, when we somehow got onto the subject of Minis and what a fiddly bloody thing they can be to work on. I'd already wheeled Mickey's big Honda out of my shed, where it had spent the night, so he could head off back to town straight after breakfast. In typical fashion, I'd launched into this detailed anecdote about the last time I'd had the misfortune to put a spanner on the old Issigonis masterwork. Then the rest of it came pouring out as well. Words came tumbling over each other, the way a bike does when it gets tossed down the road and you with it, cartwheeling along behind.

So Mickey sat back and took it all in, then grunted as he reached for his jacket and helmet, 'Christ, you're a mad bastard! No wonder Bev told you to piss off.'

With that, he straddled the Honda, pressed the starter button and, as the four roared into life, pulled down his visor, gave me a vague salute and was gone. Soon the Honda was a swiftly moving, garishly coloured dot on the thin black ribbon of road curving its way between the sentinel gums.

I wandered back inside for another coffee. I'd set it all in motion myself, of course, my year of living dangerously. The year I went off to the Isle of Man, to see the giants of motorcycle racing for the first time. A mad burst of self-indulgence, you might say. I had two excuses, good ones, I reckoned. If you call making a teenage dream come true an excuse, then that was one. But, as they used to say back in the dead days of the insurance world I once inhabited, the proximate cause was Nicko's funeral.

I remember standing with the others, my peers, at the open graveside as the December sun beat down upon our bowed heads, the stiffly arrayed 'floral tributes' already beginning to wilt, like good intentions on New Year's Day. The priest was droning on with all the old, forlorn clichés while I could only focus on the fact of Nicko's one-off heart attack. He was about my age. As far as I knew, there was no previous history. He'd always kept himself in good shape and he didn't smoke. Christ, I could be talking about myself!

I'd never been one for goal setting. It was easy enough to drift in and out of jobs and relationships in those palmy days. Things began to change when Bev got her hooks into me. The old familiar story. No, it wasn't a case of have to, although that was only blind luck. You simply drifted into marriage, or at least I did. Next thing you know, the years are flashing by at a rate of knots and you're looking down at a mate's coffin. Well, stuff it! At least I could do the one thing I'd always wanted to do, before it was too late. I started the wheels in motion the very next day. Bev was not amused when I told her that I was off to Manxland via London, early in June. Ticket booked along with solo accommodation at the Athol pub in Douglas. My treat. My life. Not hers to share.

So, burying the hurt, she quietly followed suit and made her own decisions and strategic dispositions, unbeknown to me. Mind you, I did tilt the board a little to help matters along. She and Maurie were of a kind; I felt they deserved each other. So did our friendly neighbour, Jan, when she noticed what I was up to with my bit of social engineering. We both encouraged their conjunction, as the opportunities arose in our loose grouping of friends. The chickens, of course, came roosting home eventually.

We'd made love one Sunday morning with easy familiarity, releasing some of the niggling tensions of last night's dinner party. Bev must have sensed Jan's hand eagerly seeking my receptive crotch under the table after we'd drained the third bottle of red. Maurie, true to form, was responding to Bev's every word, like a dutiful knight errant.

'Do you love me?' Bev asked after we'd rolled apart, sated, and returned to our neutral corners of the marital bed.

Mind you, our sex together was always pretty good. Funny it was never enough. What do you say to that, I thought.

'Well?' she persisted.

'Sometimes,' was my ill-considered response.

Bev was ready for me. 'I think it's time you moved out,' she said flatly. And that was it.

Later that morning, while I was still kidding myself that I'd got what I really had wanted for years, there was a brief knock on the front door. It was Matt, our burly, weather-beaten neighbour from across the road. Bev's stupid cross-bred Merino had ripped its guts open on Matt's barbed-wire fence, probably a couple of days ago. Nothing else to be done except to put it out of its misery. I loaded the .22 repeater's magazine and went looking.

Half an hour later, I finally had her bailed up in a far corner of the paddock. The pale tentacles oozing from her gashed side were already fly-blown. She'd calmed down at the sound of my voice and I was able to get close enough to grab the end of the piece of clothesline Bev used to lead her around. I gently put the muzzle of the rifle against the black wool at the nape of the neck and pulled the trigger. Then twice more before the thing finally dropped. Great day!

I moved out next morning, to a mate's tiny flat in town. No phone. No TV. No stereo. Not even a bloody radio. Funsville!

Over the next couple of weeks, the doubts came flooding in. Christ, all those years together! I'd even forgotten how to cook. Washing clothes was never my scene, especially by hand in the kitchen sink.

Then, one Sunday morning, Bev dropped by. She looked good enough to eat and I felt some of the old desire return as she turned her head and my kiss landed on her smooth cheek. I put the kettle on as she made a brief inspection of the untidy flat and brushed her arm apologetically as I swept dirty shirts and underwear into the wardrobe.

Bev wanted a favour, pretty please. She and Maurie were off to Kangaroo Island at the end of the week, for a few days' camping with the old gang. Would I mind house-sitting. Why not? At least it would get me out of the 4x4 dump I'd managed to manoeuvre myself into, if only for a while.

I drank too much rough red with an old mate on Thursday night, so I was a bit the worse for wear next morning, although a long, hot shower helped to get me moving. I dumped a few things in a bag and took off in the ancient Ford. I was actually whistling along with a familiar tune on the just-functioning radio, when I saw them heading towards me down the old Norton Summit road. They were in Maurie's shiny new Toyota.

Suddenly I was as jealous as all hell. It was bloody weird, the way all the old fairy tales about being faithful until death us do part came spinning into my now pounding skull. By the time I nosed the Cortina down the rutted driveway and pulled up alongside the dark bulk of our home, Bev's and mine, salty tears were streaming down my cheeks. Luckily, I found half a bottle of Scotch in the bar cupboard and collapsed with it on the spare bed. I couldn't bring myself to climb into our big old four-poster, with the lingering trace of Bev's favourite perfume still evident.

The magpies woke me before dawn with their carolling. I decided to give up the unequal struggle and groaned my way to the shower. The bathroom was in a well-remembered state of terminal chaos, but the hot water service was still functioning. I scrambled a couple of eggs from the fridge and was part-way through my second slice of toast when the phone jangled my jumpy nerve endings. When I was still working, I'd organised an 1100 motor for my son Tim's 850 Mini. Bev had told him where to find me and since the thing was sitting there in the shed, how about he shot up so we could swap them over? I loved that 'we' garbage. Tim could strum his guitar with the best of them, but put a spanner in his lily whites! Still, it might take my mind of his mother for a bit, and besides, it was a chance to spend time with the kid. Do us both a favour, of course. It was a while since I'd last done any mechanical work, but it's like riding a bike: you never forget, do you?

Tim eventually appeared and we skirted our way past recent history while rolling the Mini over the pit. The cover boards were set in place with a seal of ancient grease and had to be prised up with a pinch bar. There was an inch or two of black, oily water in the bottom and we took it in turns to bail out the smelly brew. Tim, in his typical absent-minded fashion, had already wiped greasy fingers on his white T-shirt.

The old engine unit came out with relative ease, thanks to my ancient block and tackle. Then the fun began. I was only half with it. My mind kept wandering back over the years. My life with Bev, the kids, the once-upon-a-time dreams, and now she was on that other island, with that prick Maurie. I felt like the Mini's engine, turning slowly this way and that as it dangled on the end of the chain.

Tim broke into my reverie of bitter thoughts. He was down in the pit, trying to marry up mountings that refused to cooperate.

I climbed stiffly down to join him. 'Where's the bloody leadlight? I complained. 'How do you expect me to see anything in this fucking black hole?'

Poor Tim, great choice of an old man he'd made. When he passed me the light, the sickly fumes from the oil-spattered globe reminded me of long days, and longer nights, spent toiling on other people's cars. I retched, wiping bile-tasting lips with the back of my unclean hand.

'Fucking typical,' I growled.

Tim winced. Nobody likes to hear their own father swear.

'Nothing ever fits. I'll have to remake the engine mounts. Lucky the bloody arc welder's still here.'

It went on like that throughout the rest of that dreary afternoon. Eventually we washed our blackened hands in some equally dirty kero and wiped them in silence on an old, torn sheet. At least the new engine fired up without too much trouble and I gave it a bit of a squirt, down to the village and back.

Tim said little but gripped the sides of his seat with knuckles that were white under the grime. He declined my offer of a scratch meal, but patted me on the shoulder with a brief, 'Thanks, mate. See yah soon.'

The Mini spun gravel from its near-bald front tyres as the bigger motor responded to the demands of Tim's accelerator foot. I turned on my heel when the red flicker of the brake lights told me he'd reached the main road.

I'd knocked off Bev's scotch last night, but there were still a few bottles of red in what I used to laughingly call my 'cellar'. The local shiraz had aged well. It helped to improve the can of baked beans I'd discovered in the pantry, hiding behind a pile of old newspapers. All the while, my mind kept hammering away on the same old theme of remorse and regret.

I couldn't shake the images of Bev and Maurie, going at it in our old tent. Over and over, like a silent movie replaying itself, the flickering frames kept queuing up in front of my eyes. The tent nestled in the dunes, with the gulls wheeling silently overhead and the moon already on the rise, like a great silver medallion, hanging there, watching the shadows moving.

I reached for the phone. Yes, there was an early morning flight to KI. Luckily, there was a small amount of credit left on the plastic. Until the house sold and we did the split up that I now kept thinking I didn't want, I had little cash to my name.

Red-eyed, I parked the Cortina and dragged myself over to the terminal. One thing about airports, at least you can get a drink twenty-four hours a day, at a price. A couple of breakfast Bloody Marys slid down easily, and I felt marginally alive again as we taxied out to the runway.

The hazy outline of the island soon appeared beneath the port wing. The chequerboard pattern of crops and paddocks sprang into focus as the cumulus parted to make way for our descent.

As far as I could tell, Kingscote didn't seem to have changed much in the few years since I was there last. The aging blonde in the Rent-A-Car office even remembered me from the old days. She gave me her standard come-on smile, which we both knew signified bugger all, but made the punters feel good. The tired Commodore was all she had left. With four almost treadless Michelins, it wouldn't have got a licence tick in Adelaide. No matter. At least it started and ran without blowing too much smoke.

I had no idea were Bev and her crowd were camped, but it had to be on the coast, so I mentally tossed a coin. It came down heads, so I took off on a clockwise circuit. Christ! Those fucking ball-bearing roads! Brake, tippy-toed, now just a gentle dab in a straight line. Use the transmission lever like a manual, put the boot in. Get the tail out, that's more like it. The old rally driving instincts took over and, for a moment or two, I actually started enjoying myself. But then it seemed in no time at all I was back where I'd started from, with unbidden tears of frustration and rage blurring my vision.

I hastily bought a tinny of beer for lunch and left some of the remaining rubber on the last of the hot bitumen in my haste to start the second circuit.

Late in the afternoon, peering through the sand-blasted windscreen into the fast-sinking sun, I spotted a narrow sandy track heading off through the dunes towards the sea. There were fresh tyre marks. I felt a sudden surge of adrenalin. Surely my luck had turned this time. Nosing the Commodore around a blind bend, I braked sharply as a cluster of tents appeared on my left, scattered around the shoreline. Bingo!

Blindly I headed for the familiar blue and yellow dome and parted the flap. Bev and Maurie looked up at me in disbelief. Maurie spilled playing cards onto the check rug, from fingers suddenly affected with palsy. It was as if I'd appeared from outer space, in a cylinder of blue light.

I almost yelled in triumph, 'Thanks for beaming me up, Scotty.'

Jan's two kids were in one corner, but no Jan. She was the last person I wanted to see.

'Bev, I'd like to talk to you. Will you come out to the car? Please?'

She hesitated for a moment then climbed awkwardly to her feet, gave Maurie a slight grimace and, with a shrug, slipped through the opening.

Outside, the first stars were beginning to appear as the sky darkened. I wound the windows up and turned sideways to look at Bev. She studiously avoided my gaze while carrying out a microscopic examination of her fingernails.

'Well,' she breathed coolly, 'this is a turn up for the books.'

I stammered. 'You and me, the kids, all those years together, we can't let it go to waste. Come back with me tonight. We'll make a fresh start. Sell the house. Move interstate. Anything you say.'

Bev looked up at me, shook her head wearily and sighed in a way that said it all. She could have just let it go at that. Instead, she spelled it out for me. In her book, it was long over, a lost cause. And yes, it went way back. Even before my solo jaunt to that other island, although that was the clincher. Forget it, mate. On your bike and leave me with my faithful friends.

I headed the Commodore back towards Kingscote with the familiar hollow emptiness in my gut. Now it had company: a blinding, tension headache that started at the back of my neck, ran through the top of my skull and was trying to get out from behind my smarting eyes.

Luckily, the pub had a room, even if everything else in the place was closed. I made do with strong black tea liberally laced with sugar and broke open the small, sanitised pack of sweet biscuits. A long, hot shower helped unknot some of my aches and partly eased my thumping head, but sleep refused to come.

I was first into the dining room at breakfast and my stomach welcomed everything I shovelled down. There were real carnations on the tables and the view out over the bay was superb. I promised myself that one day, when all the shit had cleared from my life, I would return, order a leisurely breakfast and actually enjoy the sunlight shimmering on the sky-blue sea.

I dropped the dust-streaked Commodore at the terminal building and shuffled aboard the Fokker with a sprinkling of bleary-eyed fellow travellers.

Back at the flat, my headache had finally given best to a handful of analgesics when the newly connected phone rang. The strident clamour jolted me out of my self-pitying stupor. It was Tim. He was in casualty at the Royal Adelaide with his current partner, Tania. He was OK, just a bit shaken up. They had thought at first that Tania had a broken hip, but the X-rays indicated otherwise. Could I give them a lift home to Unley? Some old guy in a Valiant had asserted his right of way in a nearby back street. Tim hadn't seen him until Tania screamed, and by then it was too late. The Mini, of course, was totalled.

I put down the phone and climbed wearily into the old Cortina.

Wiradjuri Country

An early Friday lunch and we began our journey with an easy drive to Mildura, well in time for any happy hour that may have been on offer. On the outskirts of the sprawling metropolis, an anonymous cabin in a quite well wooded caravan park suited us fine. Back into the main drag, the long-suffering Honda smoothed its way through the bunched-up four-wheel drives and raucous utes. We found a parking spot and joined the assorted throngs heading for their favourite eateries. A moving book launch mob – the local literati – had taken over the now too-well-known restaurant of our choice.

We moved purposefully on, since lunch was now a distant memory, and soon found a suitable Italian alternative, albeit no less busy, but well organised. The swarthy young waiter smiled us to a tucked-away table for two and soon returned, still smiling, with our bottle of Adelaide Hills Merlot. He proffered it for our approval then deftly removed foil and cork, poured a small amount in my glass and, with my nod, filled both our glasses above the mark. He politely agreed with my hopeful observation that at least some vintners would continue the tradition of using corks to seal their reds.

We were soon sipping the Merlot with garlic focaccia fingers, followed by pizza pescatore with a crisp Italian salad. Jane plumped for her favourite dessert – affogato, with fra angelico the liqueur. I chose an espresso with grappa. This latter revived distant memories of now long-vanished Calabrian workmates who'd first introduced me to the delights of the Mediterranean diet, including their fiery homemade version of the distiller's art.

Once outside again, the night air was noticeably warmer and the noise level kept rising as the rate of emptying the jugs of beer passing along the crowded tables lining the footpaths increased exponentially. The natives, not to say the tourists, were becoming noticeably restless, and the hitherto unmarked police presence became suddenly visible as the familiar chequerboard patterns fluoresced under flashing blue lights on patrol cars taking up station at each end of the mall. We decided it was already past our bedtime and beat a strategic retreat.

With little to pack, we were underway early on Saturday morning, heading north-east across the dreary Hay Plains, God awful country, inhospitable, hot, dry and dusty, the adjectives that always spring to mind. The flat, monotonous landscape could be terra nullius, if it wasn't for the tight black ribbon of bitumen and the occasional trio of road trains heading down south from Sydney, travelling nose to tail in consideration of other road users, of course.

Unmemorable small decaying townships appeared from time to time, shimmering in the heat haze. A source of momentary annoyance at the ludicrous fifty kilometre an hour speed limit, ignored at the peril of some zealous lurking plod with much-fondled radar gun always at the ready. A necessary coffee stop at the eponymous town itself: the usual rural Oz sprawl – plenty of fucking land, mate, no need to crowd together like niggers in a woodpile.

At least the bakery boasted a proper coffee machine and the lass operating it was competent, even ventured a smile. Caffeine levels topped up, we bathed once more in the car's air con. Predictably, there was no servo on our way out of town so, fingers crossed, I assumed there would be a bowser at Goolgowi. Luckily the Honda eats the metric miles frugally and we refilled at a price then pushed on for another hour and more until West Wyalong provided sufficient shade for a late picnic lunch. We weren't keen enough to search the other points of the compass for the other Wyalongs, assuming they exist.

Remember the schoolyard myths about this nation of sun-bronzed warriors, horny-handed sons and daughters of toil who acknowledged no boss as better and shrugged off any yoke of tyranny? Well, like all myths, today's reality is somewhat different, trust me. Let one relevant example illustrate my point. In the false name of road safety, this nation of travellers endures an ever-changing barrage of speed limits. This was brought home to me as we travelled, same road, same topography, same conditions, but one minute we can legally travel at a hundred and ten kilometres an hour, the next we're down to a hundred. Work that out. I can't. Of course, that's only the tip of the iceberg. I won't bother you with all the other nonsense. Suffice to say that serious motorists from Europe, where they invented the internal combustion engine and understand high-speed driving as an art form, must shake their collective heads in disbelief.

But, I digress. Returning to the journey: some eight hundred plus kilometres later, we arrive in Dubbo, our destination, to thirty-five-degree heat. The motel on the main drag has a pool, surrounded by a sea of bubbling bitumen, bereft of even a single shade tree. Pioneer country this. Welcome to interstate road travel in twenty-first-century Orstraya.

A Day At Henley Beach

It was one of the typical long hot summers of my pre-teen years. Our mother had bundled me with my sister aboard the tramcar after we'd trudged across the open paddocks to the main road. We were already hot and thirsty, with no relief likely until we met up with aunts and cousins sheltering under the jetty at Henley Beach.

The tram rattled across the viaduct with a good deal of clattering and groaning from the heat-distorted timber framework around the windows and elsewhere. The cacophony of noises signalled the halfway mark in what now seemed an interminable journey. I must have dozed off for a while but suddenly jolted back to reality when a screech of brakes signalled our arrival at the terminus on Military Road.

Mum thrust our old grey rug at me. 'Here, make yourself useful for a change. Carry the rug.' She had our sandwiches and some of her apple pie wrapped up in greaseproof paper and a brown paper bag stowed in her shopping bag, with a small thermos of tea.

We climbed down from the tram and made our way across the bare, hot concrete, then down the wooden steps to the even hotter sand of the beach. The cool shade under the jetty beckoned and there, spread out on a scatter of rugs, were three of Mum's sisters and, as I blinked my eyes into focus, several of my cousins, including Meg. Meg was a year older than me and good fun; we always seemed to gravitate together.

At her instigation, we'd already started to explore each other's body when circumstances permitted, a sort of advance form of 'doctors and nurses' we'd played a few years before. I'd, as yet, been unable to rise to the occasion, but that hadn't stopped Meg from grabbing my cock and rubbing it between her legs at our last fleeting encounter.

My priority at that moment, however, was to cool off in the calm waters of the gulf. Up behind the rugs, in the darker recess of the jetty, one of the aunts had put up a smallish square tent of faded, striped canvas. Nobody seemed near it, so I thought to slip inside and change into my bathers. I pulled open the flap and made to enter its semi-darkness, but a voice stopped me dead in my tracks. Then I made out the bulky form of my Auntie Gemma, with her top open and my latest baby cousin sucking noisily on one of her big white breasts.

'I think you'd better run back to the others, dear, while I finish feeding little Andrew, that's the boy.'

I stammered an apology and, red-faced, beat a hasty retreat.

I hastily took off my shirt, grabbed a towel from Mum's bag, wound it around my waist and quickly shed shorts and underpants, then slipped on my bathers using the towel to protect my modesty. The water was still cold enough to take my breath away, but I soon got used to it and decided to head out further, leaving my sister and younger cousins paddling in the shallows. I looked for Meg and saw her a little way off, madly having a splashing fight with her younger sister.

The water was calm and I waded out parallel to the jetty, then veered towards it to avoid a bunch of older boys swimming towards me. I'd been away from school with measles when the learn-to-swim campaign started and I'd only made it to the last lesson, so I missed out and couldn't even dog paddle. Probably because of this, I just kept on walking and soon found the water lapping around my chin. I must have been daydreaming or something and had just started to turn around to head for the shore, when suddenly the firm sand gave way beneath me.

I knew immediately that I'd fallen into one of the old piling holes alongside the jetty. Some other kids had told me about them last summer and I'd forgotten until now. I plunged down into the depths then my body's buoyancy shot me up to the surface in a big tube of foam and bubbles. I knew I was in big trouble, but it was as if I was detached from myself, almost an onlooker. Down I went again, but this time when I bobbed up like a cork from a bottle, I managed to get an arm up, out of the water. I remember hoping that someone would see me before it was too late.

I was rapidly running out of breath and choking on salt water on the way down for the third time, when I felt a pair of hands grabbing and turning me on to my back. Then I was being towed back to the safety of the shore, coughing and spluttering, but alive. My rescuer helped me to stand up and when I saw his face I realised it was Uncle Ralph, Auntie Gemma's husband.

He made sure I could stand unaided then said he was on duty as a lifesaver and had to get back to his post at the end of the jetty. 'Tell your mum what happened and I'll be back as soon as I finish my shift.'

Still coughing up seawater, I shivered my way back to where Mum sat next to the others.

She thrust a towel at me. 'Here, dry yourself. Don't drip water all over the rug. Where have you been?'

I didn't know what to say, just stood there trying to rub myself dry, teeth chattering and blue in the face.

'Come on, answer me.'

I seemed to have lost the power of speech.

With that, Mum hauled off and slapped me in the face.

I burst into tears and pee ran down my still-wet legs.

Just then, I heard Uncle Ralph's voice and he towered over me for a second then squatted down alongside Auntie Gemma. He took in the scene at a glance, including the red marks on my cheek, along with the tears. He told Mum how he'd dived off the jetty and rescued me, but all she could say was how stupid I'd been for walking out so far.

Auntie Gemma leaned across and handed me my clothes from the rug and another dry towel. 'Here, love, you go up to the tent and get yourself dry and into your clothes, have a bit of a lie down. We'll call you when lunch is ready.'

I made my unsteady way over to the tent and crawled inside. Once I was dry and in my clothes, I started to feel a bit better. I lay down on the rug and soon drifted off to sleep.

After a while, I woke to feel someone stroking my face. It was Meg.

She put her arms around me and whispered, 'Gawd! Your mum's a bitch, isn't she? Anyway, never mind. Here's something to cheer you up.' With that she hoisted up her top, took my hand and placed it on her bare breast. 'Haven't they grown since last time? Here, give us your other hand. Feel them both.'

I hastened to obey. They felt so good, firm and smooth like two small torpedoes. They seemed to float in space, both angled away from the centre of Meg's chest, just beautiful.

I've never forgotten that particular day at Henley, my narrow escape from drowning and my mother's reaction, but most of all I can still visualise Meg proudly showing me her tits (as I would have called them at the time), thereby making me feel that life was worth living after all. Meg and I were never on such intimate terms again. She soon went off to boarding school and the next time we met was at her wedding, then the newly weds moved interstate.

My mother always rubbished my rescuer, Uncle Ralph. Although he was fit enough to be a volunteer lifesaver, he lived on the invalid pension and continued to get Auntie Gemma pregnant. No sooner had she weaned one baby than she'd be in the family way again. Eventually she produced ten kids and Mum never forgave Uncle Ralph. He was supposed to have really bad arthritis and Mum said, 'There's only one place he's got it. Pity it didn't bloody well fall off.' Auntie Gemma may well have agreed!

Prunes and Sago

It turned out to be Flo's last Christmas with us. She actually hung on for several more years, but we went to her subsequently – a considerable relief, I might add. I'd given in again and said we'd have her down for a few days. This meant driving up to town and out to her western suburbs unit. The same drive I'd been doing for thirty years or more. She and Cyril George, my late father, moved in to their original, upstairs two-bedroom unit in the retirement 'village' before he'd even officially retired at sixty five. Some 'village'. Not even a common room, let alone a community barbecue.

Cyril George had a small, round aluminium barbecue with three screw-in tubular legs. He kept this trophy tucked away in its original cardboard case under the stairs, along with a small supply of split deal in a hessian bag. Where he'd found the wood in that sterile suburban wilderness remained a mystery. Sometimes on a Sunday, if the weather was kind, he would set up the barbecue on a stretch of pavement by the stairs and cook a few sausages with sliced onion and potato for their lonely lunch. By the time Cyril George had laboured up the stairs with his burnt offerings, Flo would have opened a can of beetroot and emptied the contents into a patterned glass bowl formerly the property of her mother. The beetroot was always accompanied by shredded iceberg lettuce and wedges of tomato, the lettuce dressed with a sprinkle of sugar and a squeeze of lemon. They ate in the cramped kitchen/dining space, deemed sufficient for two pensioners by the 1960s architects responsible for diminishing the lives of those so accommodated.

Almost immediately after Cyril George met his solitary end, from dementia, in a hospice designed by the same architects, two bus trips away, Flo was quickly moved into a downstairs single bedroom unit as befitted her widowed status. No longer could she look down on her neighbours. To make matters worse, the usual renovations were deferred while their old unit was gutted, cleansed, repainted and modernised. No doubt the ever-friendly management team expected Flo to follow Cyril George's example and shuffle off within a shortish space of time.

No such luck. She was made of sterner stuff and chose to linger on, making life as difficult as she could for those within her orbit. Her lifelong ambition, to live in a house with a flagpole, would now never be fulfilled. I never did think to ask what flag she favoured – although the skull and crossbones did come to mind on more than one occasion. Inevitably, I found myself driving on automatic pilot on my way to pick up Flo, while all the familiar images of the above, their most recent history, were plucked from the filing cabinet of my brain and endlessly displayed.

I was late, of course – well, later than she'd expected me to arrive. It was ever thus. Fortunately for me, this meant that her ancient small suitcase was packed and ready to go, while the lady herself had trotted out one of her better ensembles for the occasion. She finished off a row of knitting, stuffed wool and needles into a carry bag and announced herself ready for departure.

The drive to my home took about an hour and a half. I was in no mood for conversation, preferring to concentrate on the task of driving. Flo, however, was never one to waste a silence. She began her usual litany: had I heard from my sister? Neither had she – 'Wouldn't think I had a family.' I'd long since refrained from pointing out the obvious; of course, it was my sister she wanted, not me, and Caroline had no wish to play the dutiful daughter while I was around to fetch and carry. Rather like the Australian terrier we'd briefly enjoyed years ago, until Flo gave it away to a passing stranger because she didn't like animals, couldn't bear to touch them. Caroline could never forgive and forget; bit like her mother really. Truth be known, Caroline was a clone of Flo, but nether of them could see it.

While I mused, the litany continued: 'Why don't you shave that thing off your face. Iit makes you look too old.' (I'd had a beard for at least thirty years at that time.)

Somewhere in her past, Flo had developed a phobia against bearded men. On one occasion, in the absence of her smarmy, smooth-skinned Asian GP, the surgery had sent a locum to attend to one of Flo's panic ailments at home. He was a rather large young man with, as luck would have it, a well cultivated bushy beard. Flo refused to let him near her and abused poor Cyril George for even letting the hapless chap enter their unit. I never did find out who, or what, had triggered her phobia and, at the time, Cyril George hadn't a clue either.

Fortunately she'd lapsed into silence by the time I pulled under our carport and ushered her inside the house.

Flo was no longer an early riser and my wife, June, had already gone off to work before this apparition appeared in the kitchen doorway. Flo always seemed to have reasonable outfits to wear when she went out. On occasion, for a woman in her nineties, she could still appear quite smart. Her night attire was a different story. I was a touch embarrassed when I looked up from my muesli and saw her standing there in that tatty, ancient nightie. No, she only had an old winter dressing gown, formerly my father's.

I fished around in one of June's wardrobes and found a floral number I hadn't seen for years. 'Time for breakfast, Mum.' I produced a new box of generic Weetbix from the pantry and a packet of dried prunes; Flo's breakfast of choice for decades.

Sadly, she preferred her prunes stewed with sago. 'Why'd you buy these things?' she questioned querulously.

'Sorry, Mum, we don't run to sago, so you'll just have to make do.

I'll leave you to it now. I have to get the car serviced. Back in a couple of hours.'

In fact, I'd arranged to meet a couple of mates at the bowling club for a couple of quick ends and an early beer or two. Well, it was Christmas after all, and there was no way I intended to spend my leisure hours listening to Flo complain about her aches and pains if I could possibly avoid it. The sun was over the yardarm somewhere when we settled into position at the bar and sucked gratefully on our first round of coldies.

The conversation soon switched from bowls to local gossip and then I mentioned Flo's presence at our Christmas festivities. It seemed I was not alone in having to put up with an old biddy.

Harry was first cab off the rank. 'Christ almighty,' he declaimed, 'you think you've got problems. I'm stuck with Thelma's Ma, me mother-in-law, the original whingeing Pom. If she's not complaining about something, she's bloody well asleep!'

Ted nodded, drained his schooner and said, 'Come on, you pricks, it's my buy. Last round then I've got to go.'

Charlie, the barman, set up three fresh beers and joined the conversation as he rinsed and dried the empties. 'Reckon I'm lucky. My oldies are long gone and the old lady pissed off to Queensland years ago; lives with my sister and her useless brood. So I'm on me own most of the time.' He winked.

We smiled. Charlie had a good thing going with an older bird from the pub, to their mutual benefit. She wasn't all that bad, we'd each agreed, lucky bastard.

'Only problem I've got,' he continued, 'these bloody end of year family newsletters. The sister prints off a whack and posts them to all the old rellies who aren't on the fucken net. Just listen to this crap.' He pulled a crumpled sheet of A4 paper out of his top pocket, poured himself a small beer and began reading. 'I'll skip the opening twaddle, but there's a couple of bits you'll like. 'Course, I don't even know who she's fucken talking about half the time. They all breed like rabbits up there, must be the water or something. Get this: "Sharlize is now eight and has ballet lessons every week." Sharlize: where do they get these fucken names from? "She's so good at it her teacher says she's best in the class. She can do the splits like you wouldn't believe. Jack picks her up, stands her on his shoulders and down she goes, like a flash. Seems to float somehow, like a swan and as she lands just stretches out her legs and does the splits."' Charlie paused and shuddered at his mental picture.

We three looked at each other and then Charlie. I'm sure we had each felt the same instinctive tightening in our balls.

Sensing our mutual reaction, Charlie read another excerpt from his treasure trove of banality. "'Dallas is the local skateboarding star. He's only small, but he's ever so clever. You should see what he can do on the local council ramp. It's just bad luck he broke his arm last week. Wouldn't you know with Christmas and all that? It wasn't his fault one of the little wheel things busted and he came down hard on the edge of the concrete. He's been so brave, a real example to us all. Jack thinks we might have a claim against the skateboard makers; he's going to talk to someone he knows in consumer affairs.'"

'Yeah, well, thanks, Charlie, for sharing that with us,' I ventured, wiped my mouth with the back of my hand and set the empty glass back on the bar. 'I'm off, see you blokes later.'

Back at the ranch, Flo was still sitting at the kitchen table in her nighty and June's dressing gown, reading the paper.

She gave me a look of triumph. 'I found the sago.'

I rocked back on my heels.

'I can't believe how much stuff she's got in that pantry, never heard of half of it. What she need all that for?'

'June likes to cook,' I responded stiffly, hackles rising.

'Anyway, I found a jar full. Wasn't labelled, though. I think she should label things. Funny sort of stove you've got. Took me ages to find any matches in this place. Then I couldn't work out how to turn the gas on. It's all back to front to mine.'

'Mum, you just press the little red button, its electronic – I showed that last time you were here.'

'Well, at least I finally had my breakfast with proper prunes stewed with sago, the only way I like them. I'm sorry about the saucepan. After I dished myself some prunes, I put the saucepan back on the stove and forgot to turn off the gas.'

'So that's what I can smell. Thanks, Mum. Merry Christmas.'

Monologue and Triangle

Can I get you anything, Kate? Coffee? Wine? No, you're sure? OK. Fine.

I'm so glad you agreed to meet me like this. It's been too long since we've had a chance to talk. One on one, that is.

Jim's been gone now, what, five years? So we've known each other for over ten, more than a decade! Where did all that time go?

Um, where to start? I guess, really, for me, it's about wanting to feel closer to you. I mean, back when Jim was still alive – must be, what, six seven years ago, remember – we used to meet on the bike track. Ride to the cove for coffee and a chat. Every Tuesday, rain or shine! I used to look forward to that.

Then later, when you and Helen worked together and became bosom buddies, things changed. For me, that is. The closer you two became, the further away that left me, I was on the outer, well and truly. No! No! I'm not complaining, I'm just trying to explain my position. It's great that you two are such good friends. My two favourite women.

But I just feel, um, I just feel I'm too much on the outer. I mean, I'd like to feel we were back closer, the way we used to be. You're very special to me, you know. Yes, yes, I know you feel that way about me too. That's what I need to hear. And it's not really a physical thing. Not really.

I mean, we've always given each other a decent hug and a peck on the cheek and that's fine. I remember the time when we actually had the occasional full on kiss on the lips. Even a bit of a tonguey!

No, I know you decided we'd better stop and I know Helen still reacts when I give you a hug. She can't help herself, poor love, she's so insecure. But that shouldn't be our problem. Should it?

No! Please don't get me wrong. I'm not criticising Helen, that's the last thing I want to do. What I'm trying to say is… I just need to feel that we are really close to each other. It brought it home to me the other night. When you phoned Helen to say you were feeling unwell and had decided not to meet us for dinner at the Angas. Made me stop and think. What if something happened to you in the night? Stuck in that big house on your own, it'd be terrible.

I want you to promise me that if anything happens, anything at all, that you'll phone me straight away, day or night. I'm only a phone call away. I mean it, you're too important in my life.

Sorry, I guess that all sounds a bit heavy, a bit over the top. Um, but I have to say something else. I don't want you to take this the wrong way. So please don't get upset, OK? But I rather wish you hadn't told me about your married friend, in London, that time.

Sure I know what he said, or what you told me he said, about wanting a bit more than a platonic friendship with you. I mean, either a friendship's platonic or it isn't. You can't have it both ways. I just think he wanted to get into your pants, that's what I think.

OK, sorry, I know it's a fine line, and yes, I can see your point. I suppose, in a way, I'm going on about the same thing. But can't you see that for me it's not about sex. It's about feeling good with each other. It's…it's about that we're special with each other.

Sorry, sorry, Kate, I don't think I can talk about it any more, not at the moment.

Des, honey, dinner's ready. Why are you sitting out there in the dark, love? I didn't realise you were home. Then I thought I heard you on your mobile, talking to someone. But your phone's in here, on the table. I'm dishing up, love. Can you come in now? Oh! Now there's someone at the door. Just a minute, I'm coming. Desmond, darling, it's the police. They want to know whether we've seen Kate today.

The Unknown Friend

You don't know me, my friend, but I know you only too well. Do let me explain. We may well both benefit – anything is possible in this strange new world.

I'd just lowered my ancient buttocks onto the chill white plastic toilet seat, thoughtfully provided (under the requirements of the relevant act) by those caring Fresh Food people.

Mother always said, 'Never use a public toilet, dear. However, if urgent need should arise, be very sure to wipe the seat, or better still, squat, but keep your body well clear.'

'Why, Mum?'

'Because you might catch something dreadful down there, that's a good boy. Now run along.'

Well, tempus fugit, as our Latin teacher once droned. And the strangely designed prostate gland has its own imperative these days. Clutching my small green eco-friendly bag with this week's supply of baked beans and other necessities, I managed to find an empty cubicle with the seat up (thus indicating it was last used as a pissoir and not fouled by a stranger's ordure). Mine own observation over the years, not mother's, I hasten to add.

Prostate and bladder were both relieved and reluctantly accepting of whatever malignant germs were already making their rapid way towards my ineffectual immune system from their home on the white plastic toilet – no doubt heavily colonised thanks to a parsimonious cleaning contractor, already operating on the proverbial shoestring.

But I digress. My apologies – an aged pensioner's prerogative.

Sadly, I realised on reaching for the elusive end of the gossamer-thin toilet paper, that both rolls had been torn off flush with their enclosing tamper-proof covers, by you, my unknown thoughtless friend. My pulse rate immediately quickened and I broke into a cold sweat. What would Mother have thought? I took several deep breaths and endeavoured to be calm.

Minutes passed. Eventually, using the fingertips of both arthritic hands, success crowned my patient fumbling, as with great care the near priceless ends of both rolls emerged at last and, wadded to a usable thickness, suitable lengths were put to good use. Mother, I'm sure, would have approved.

Why I Hate Airports

Of all the places to be, my third wife and I fetched up at the appalling Charles de Gaulle airport. This was at the conclusion of what proved to be our last holiday together. It was, unhappily, the predictable end of a fairly brief marriage, her second, after a disastrous first. I'd galloped up on my white charger to rescue her from a relatively peaceful life with her trio of teenage delinquent children, but it all went pear-shaped, for me anyway, about the date we headed to Europe. By the time we'd got to Paris, it was separation time. The day Annie went to the Louvre I went to the d'Orsay; at least we were still on speaking terms.

We'd arrived by train from Italy, both knackered and wanting only to crash in a decent bed or beds and just sleep. For once, Lonely Planets let us down and we trudged to the nearest of their local recommendations, towing our luggage. It proved to be a real dump. Said to be recently refurbished and updated, our room, on the third floor, reached by a succession of narrow, uncarpeted stairs, had not even seen a cleaner, let alone a paintbrush, in this century. Someone had obviously vomited on the ancient strip of moth-eaten carpet gracing the landing and any attempt at cleaning up the mess had been largely unsuccessful.

This was the sorry introduction to our room. The only sign of renovation was a recently replastered and whitewashed room just along the landing, lacking a door. Our 'en suite' was hidden behind a dirty plastic curtain, only a metre from the foot of the elderly double bed, covered by a duvet that had clearly enjoyed a long and interesting life. There was, however, a fair supply of hot water, although the stained washbasin lacked a plug and the cold water tap dripped from time to time. Meals were available in house, but we decided not to risk food poisoning and instead ate out at the selection of cheap wine bars favoured by the local populace.

Somehow, we managed to survive the next few days in this rat trap. One, because it was affordable, and two, because we simply lacked the energy to search for something better in our price range, *c'est la vie!*

On the eve of our departure back to Oz, we added up our dwindling supply of francs and decided there was just enough to cover the bus trip to the airport, with a small reserve for emergencies. Are all French bus drivers selected for their suicidal tendencies, I wondered? Anyway, we obviously made it in one piece. Perhaps the saints were on our side for once.

I seem to recall that the Charles de Gaulle was hailed at the time of its completion as a wonderful example of space-age architecture. Airports, in my experience, are the last places on Earth that human beings should be required to spend any time. Like supermarket car parks, they are designed by seriously deranged individuals who, quite clearly, never use the end products of their warped minds. The Charles de Gaulle is a prize example of this metier, a huge covered space, rather like an oversize football stadium, with the necessary bits and pieces to sustain life jammed higgledy-piggledy in the middle.

We instantly recognised all the wonderful worldwide franchises; it was just like home. Around the distant walls were an array of giant tubes, stacked one on top of the other and pointing upwards at an angle towards the heavens. These tubes are the means of delivery by which the subdued passengers gain access to their respective aeroplanes, drained by coping with the sheer complexity of the place.

We'd ascertained that we were not required to board our flight until five a.m. at the earliest, so the long night stretched ahead of us. A miniature bottle of three-star cognac had somehow found its way into my backpack. We managed to find the bar and were relieved to note that it boasted on remaining open twenty-four-seven, thanks be to the small gods of French airports. Sitting back in a brace of comfortable lounge chairs we shared the cognac into our glasses of ice and soda water and attempted to relax.

Later, we abandoned our scruples and dined à la Burger King for the first and, as far as I was concerned, the only time, using the plastic. Two double cheeseburgers, a serve of 'French' fries – cold by the time we ate them, one number three salad, plus two beers in, of course, plastic cups; although to be fair, the best measure yet in our Parisian experience. All for only 95.04 francs. An overnight cocoon would have cost us three hundred so we forked out fifty francs to park our cases in a locker and chose to sit up all night rather then buy more francs or to put more money on Visa.

The man with the floor polishing machine makes sure that no one sleeps, although at least he didn't try to run over me. Unlike the Yamaha-riding employee of the Paris sanitation department, riding along the footpath vacuuming up dog shit, near our hotel earlier in the day. The large North African, lying full length on a nearby pair of seats with his head resting on one of the metal arms, wore a bulky assortment of obviously cast-off clothing, topped by a misshapen woollen hat, layered with grime. Rather surprisingly, there was no cloud of flies enjoying the farmyard aroma wafting around his person. He was clearly a denizen of this place. Just around the corner sat a shopping trolley, groaning under a precarious mountain of battered suitcases, cardboard cartons and bulging plastic bags.

We guessed, rightly, that this remarkable collection belonged to our slumbering friend. After a time, he rose languidly from his repose to bludge a cigarette from a passing traveller. Puffing comfortably, he wheeled away another, less laden, trolley, which acted as a Zimmer frame to support his girth. I calculated that he was one of the at least eighty per cent of those we encountered that wearisome night smoking cigarettes and the odd cigar. I found myself musing on the perils of passive smoking and wondered just how long it would take to detoxify our systems, should we survive.

We did learn from the worn-out-looking blonde dispensing a form of coffee from a booth at some point in the wee small hours, who fortunately spoke a little English, that the trolley-toting giant hailed from Algeria. Sadly, he had arrived at the Charles de Gaulle some years earlier lacking the necessary paperwork. He was found to be stateless and now, it seemed, doomed to spend the rest of his life wandering within the confines of this monstrous prison.

All in all, as you may have gathered, I did not find much to enjoy, for me in not-so-gay Paree.

I will draw a veil over the rest of this night, the flight home and then all the joys of finalising and formalising the end of that particular marriage. I want to move on to tell you about the second of my worst airport experiences.

The important thing to know about our modern armoury of medicinal drugs is that they all have side effects. This was brought home to me the hard way in 2014, my personal *annus horribilis*. After enjoying a long run of comparatively good health, I was suddenly in a lot of pain. I won't dwell on the boring details; suffice to say that a blood test revealed to my friendly GP that I was suffering from a not uncommon ailment called poly-something. One of the drugs prescribed was cortisone-based and I was put on a fairly high dosage for rather too long and became quite manic.

The positive side of this was that I felt ten feet tall; my ego and my self-confidence hit new heights. I knew what I wanted to do and it was full steam ahead, never mind the shoals and rapids lying in wait. On the downside, initially because of the pain, I could no longer ride my beloved Ducati Monster. I couldn't even bear the thought of having to don a crash helmet; it looked as if my motorcycling days were finally behind me.

Not to worry, I thought, I'll buy a sports car. I could still drive, after a fashion, so what the hell! One last toy it was. I settled on a Mazda MX5 for various reasons, including the unfond memory of an old MG that swore me off Pommy shit for life. There were a number of Mazdas for sale on the net, but the only candidate with low miles on the clock lived in Port Lincoln, a fair way from home. This is where the overdose of cortisone kicked in, after the remnant of normality dismissed the idea of bussing to Lincoln. I got back on the computer and booked the first flight I could and organised an old mate to drop me at the Adelaide airport a day or so later.

Now, let me hasten to tell any of you who have so far not made it to this fair state, the Adelaide drome is nothing like the Charles de Gaulle I dwelt at length on earlier. Save in one respect, which I found to my cost: a detail of design that confirms my theory as outlined above. Let me explain:

In spite of a continuing program of additions and other titillations, the basic configuration remains the same: a long, split-level rectangle. The aircraft are lined up on the southern side, noses into the terminal building, for all the world like a row of feeding sharks. Passengers flying with the big operators are mainly loaded and alight via a system of large, semi-portable covered ramps. Customers of the smaller shows, catering for less popular country destinations, are required to brave the elements and walk across the tarmac to their waiting aircraft.

Sir James dropped me at the entrance to the terminal in plenty of time for my flight and I soon dropped my wheeled case with the friendly baggage handling person. She also handed me my boarding pass and indicated, with a sweep of her arm and some verbal instructions, just where I would find the right departure point. All of this, of course, went in one ear and rapidly out the other, wherein lay the seeds of my coming disaster.

Old habits die hard. Once upon a time, I'd slaved away my days as a motor mechanic. Accordingly, I'd packed a small assortment of tools in an old camera lens bag, just in case the Mazda did the unthinkable. I fronted up at the security section with my shoulder bag, having forgotten all about the little cache of spanners and a couple of stumpy screwdrivers it contained. Fuck! The rotund shit who bade me to open my bag was in his element. I tried in vain to argue that none of the tools was in anyway capable of inflicting injury, mortal or otherwise. I was not about to let this moron confiscate my collection of hardware. So I had to leave my bag sitting there and race back to my friendly baggage person. Luckily she was completely unfazed and phoned a minion to retrieve my case from the depths of the departure zone. In a matter of minutes, it was wheeled up; she unzipped the nearest compartment and stowed the lens bag within. She also mentioned, as I turned to go, that I had only five minutes or so to check in at the boarding point.

Back at the security area, chaos still reigned, with a fresh load of passengers milling around. My shoulder bag was no longer where I had left it and none of the security lot took any notice of my appeals for help. Luckily, I then spotted the cretin who had initiated this debacle supervising a knot of his fellows on the far side of their domain. My bag was sitting on a shelf near his right elbow. I leapt across and grabbed it before he could say anything and took off for the departure zone.

Unfortunately, as it turned out, I went the wrong way, towards the high-numbered gates, having completely forgotten the number of the gate I needed. I tried getting past the empty computer terminals and down to the exit level but every door was firmly locked. By the time I'd reached the end of the line and realised my mistake, most of the departure lounges were completely devoid of people. Any airline staff had disappeared with their customers. I was in big trouble and verging on collapse.

I turned back the other way and galloped along shouting at the top of my voice, 'Fuck! Fuck!' And 'Help! Help!' Nobody of the small number of bystanders took any notice. So much for airport security! Then, further disaster, I found my way towards the departure lounges blocked by solid glass partitions. I had to turn away once again, back onto the main walkway. It seemed an eternity before I got past this screened-off section. My degree of agitation had reached an even higher level and proved that at least I didn't have a heart condition – not that I stopped to think that at the time.

Just when I'd about given up, my cries for help were answered, not by a fairy godmother, but by a lass driving one of those small tractor-like devices that scuttle around airports. She stopped and asked me what was wrong and somehow I stammered out my problem. 'Hop on,' she said, 'I'll take you right there.' I collapsed on the passenger seat and we sped off to the Port Lincoln departure point. Much to my amazement, the flight had not left and someone was still patiently calling for some idiot bearing my name to report at gate whatever-it-was.

I managed to thank my benefactor and the other staff, while producing the boarding pass, which by some miracle I'd managed not to lose. I staggered out into the sunlight and there on the oil-spotted tarmac stood the petite Saab turbo-prop, with the crew standing around, waiting for this elderly nuisance. I climbed the steps with my last ounce of energy, found the correct seat under the resigned gazes of the other passengers and strove to make myself as inconspicuous as possible for the flight to Lincoln.

I found out later that the partitioned-off area blocking my path was in fact the departure and arrival section for international travellers. I may be wrong, but I don't recall any signage that might have helped to resolve my dilemma. Surely, only in South Australia would this half-witted design be tolerated. Although, come to think of it, only recently has our Clayton's expressway to the southern suburbs been duplicated after frustrating so many motorists for so long.

The Great Denim Mystery

This report was compiled by Tobias Codger (OC1) and Michael also Codger (OC2), but no relation, funnily enough, on instructions from the Ministry of and for Consumer Affairs. After being briefed by our departmental head and his assistants, we decided to set up an observation post at the southern end of the Hay Street mall, in central Perth, capital of the Swan River settlement. We took up station at approximately 10.30 hours on Wednesday 7 April. The weather conditions were ideal for our purpose, which was in the nature of a preliminary survey.

Perhaps we need to digress at this point to provide background information germane to our task. For some time, reports had begun filtering through to the ministry of a worrying shortage of denim, a type of coarse, cotton-based blue cloth, named after the French fabric *serge de Nîmes* and originally popular in the United States for work clothing. Rather ironically, the modern version, containing a percentage of nylon, is not even particularly hard-wearing.

The original men's work trousers became known as 'jeans' and, in the way of the bizarre world of fashion, increasingly became a much sought-after item of apparel for today's 'with it' young madams. The obvious question as to why such an extremely uncomfortable and heavy item of clothing could be so successfully promoted defies a logical answer. Although ever-astute garment designers in the wake of the female sexual revolution of the 1960s and 1970s succeeded in transforming humble jeans into a female fashion statement, with names such as St Laurent and even Gucci adding the garment to their catalogues (cf. Germaine Greer, the Pill, Kinsey Report).

In earlier times, for male workers, access to the forward-placed side pockets was difficult, because of the tight waistband. At one time, manufacturers provided a fob pocket for loose change; this was completely inaccessible to average male fingers and seems to have largely disappeared.

A notable feature that undoubtedly ensured a strong following was the wholesale adoption of tight jeans by the purveyors of so-called 'pop' music. Their pelvis-thrusting antics, both on and off stage, appealed to a generation of young males and their even younger female partners. It is easy to see why the genitally well-endowed members of the lower classes would covet the tight jean, with its inbuilt codpiece (cf. cod pieces, male genitalia, rock music scene).

All of which brings us back to Hay Street and the main purpose of this report.

Observation Report

Apparently because of the strange dearth of blue denim, jeans were completely absent with regard to the many young women we sighted. They were predominantly nubile, immediately post-nubile and, dare we say it, pre-nubile. Prerequisite – a pair of long, shapely legs, preferably lightly tanned, although darker brown, even ebony black, have been noted. Instead of jeans, the current fashion decreed a very brief crutch-hugging pair of denim shorts, often fringed and worn with complete nonchalance and a considerable degree of aplomb.

The V-shape of the female genital area, lacking as it does the lumpy paraphernalia of the male counterpart, lends itself admirably to these ultra-short creations. Given the closely woven denim fabric, there is usually (in our observation), no hint of the type or even existence of any undergarment. Although, having regard to historical precedent, it may well be the case that the ubiquitous 'thong', much favoured by at least one former US president, has already found its way to the Swan River settlement (cf. Clinton Bill, Lewinsky Monica, US senate proceedings).

Many of these abbreviated shorts seemed to be home-made, perhaps evolving from the scissor-cut, jagged-edged jeans of an earlier generation. It is indeed a significant leap from the mid-thigh-length shorts worn by that tranche of the female population to the current creations. The crutch-hugging displays we observed in Hay Street were the ultimate in brevity and certainly made a statement that hardly bodes well for what may follow should present trends continue. However, social comment does not fall within our remit (cf. Jeans, flared. Jeans, skeletal).

In a variation of the overall display, a number of the young ladies were wearing shorts with the pockets turned out, rather like a pair of ears; this seemed to us a touch impracticable. One further item of note was the complete absence of any bare midriff display. Very occasionally, and only noted because OC2 and I are trained observers, was an umbilicus in evidence and then simply by chance, from the glint of sunlight on a gold or silver ring or perhaps a jewel, nestling in a convenient navel.

A further part of our brief was to mount an investigation and report on the sudden disappearance of denim from the marketplace. Rumours had been circulating for some time that the Murdoch Empire had begun buying up job lots of the material from small suppliers. There seemed to be no obvious reason for Murdoch's minions to be purchasing denim rather than newsprint. Then a dedicated Murdoch watcher, surfing the net for any overlooked morsel from the *News of the World* fallout debris, discovered a rash of emails between Rupert's office and a minor research facility in Wichita, Kansas.

Evidently, a back-room scientist had managed to perfect a process by which denim could be cheaply converted into newspaper. The cost benefits arising from this process were such that given the volume of cellulose-based newspaper consumed by Rupert's worldwide empire, the order was given to acquire, as discreetly and as cheaply as possible, the entire supply of denim wherever located on the planet. We are convinced that this action precipitated the sudden appearance of ultra-short shorts and affords yet another black mark to be added to the Murdoch escutcheon.

Given under our hands this 27th day of January in the year of our Lord 2015, OC1 and OC2 for and on behalf of the Ministry for and of Consumer Affairs (Official Seal affixed)

Menopausally Odd?

I've reached the conclusion that my dear wife is menopausal. This is the only reasonable explanation I can think of to explain some of her recent, quite out of character behaviour. Of course, I couldn't possibly raise the issue with her; we don't talk about personal, private, matters even though we've been married for all these years. Some things are better left unsaid, after all. Nevertheless, I feel the need to put down my thoughts on paper. Perhaps by doing so I will better understand her actions.

It started innocently enough when old friends called in for a catch-up coffee and asked whether we would like a worm farm. They were in the process of moving from their large marital home into a more easily manageable unit with minimal garden, hence the worm farm, or rather the potential home for a quantity of worms, was now surplus to their requirements. I had no idea what they were talking about, but Dot readily agreed that we would find a place for this treasure at the back of the shed. Between us, duly we carted this collection of circular black plastic objects to its designated resting place and there it remained.

Some months later, my lovely daughter, who, unlike her father, is an avid gardener, happened by and on her guided tour of the back garden noticed the uninhabited worm house. She exclaimed in delight to my wife that she had a fully operative worm farm that constantly supplied valuable nutrients for her very productive vegetable beds. Not only that, but she would be happy to supply a population of the little toilers along with advice on how to set the whole operation into action. Dot was immediately smitten with the whole idea and within a week or so the two could report that the worms were hard at it in their dark hideaway.

You may have noticed, of course, that nothing in this life is easy, especially when gardening is involved. Not only did the worms require scraps of specially selected vegetable matter from the compost bucket, but they also had to be carefully layered between sheets of damp newspaper. On hot days, their home, already roofed over with a sheet of my marine ply, had to be cooled frequently by a fine spray of precious water. All this for a minimal quantity of foul-smelling black liquid collected in a tin at the base of the so-called farm.

I found the whole exercise not only tedious, but of doubtful real value. I suppose it did keep the worms occupied and perhaps provided them with better living conditions than might otherwise have been the case. Certainly Dot seemed to enjoy spending a good deal of time tending to their needs and it was one way of utilising old copies of *The Advertiser*.

Now, since my lovely daughter is a sworn supporter of worm farming and an avid proselytiser, I hesitate to suggest that Dot's enthusiasm for the cause is at all misplaced, let alone odd. However, within a few months I did begin to wonder, when she began breeding, of all things, tadpoles. As a small boy, I can remember catching tadpoles in the stagnant pools that lay not far from home, after the first rains of winter had passed. I even put one or two in jars of methylated spirits, in some mistaken idea that I would become a scientist. The notion of breeding 'taddies' until they metamorphosed into frogs never entered my head. I don't think my sisters or their girlfriends ever expressed any interest in the slippery, slimy things.

We have a small pond in our eastern garden. It has, I believe, one resident 'gold' fish, although it isn't of course gold, simply the last survivor of the original batch of whatever the local pet shop happened to have to hand when we first commissioned the pond. It was, no doubt, a tad larger than its fellows and waxed fat as it gobbled up the smaller fry. The other resident is a very vocal frog, which I don't think either of us has ever seen, although Dot swears she spotted it one evening in the shadow of a lily pad. The one thing we can be sure of is that the frog is female, because every now and again a large quantity of spawn appears in certain strategic places among the water plants. Although, come to think of it, how do the eggs get fertilised? Or are frogs one of those clever species that can take turns at being either sex? I must look that up sometime.

Because Dot had been feeling a bit off colour for a few days, I wandered out onto the side veranda the other morning to put a scoop of seed out for the birds. As I turned to go back inside, I couldn't help but notice this weird lit-up thing on the wall by the door. As I looked, it changed shape from a kind of bland oval to an oval with a sort of triangular sail on top. Then it went through a whole repertoire of shapes, some with a surface like a waffle maker, others plain with little eruptions, like miniature water spouts. One moment a placid silvery surface would appear; in the next instant a miniature tsunami roiled across the still water. For the life of me, I couldn't at first work out how or where the devil it was coming from. It was quite spooky in a way, but fascinating. I sang out to Dot to come and have a look. Then as I waited for her to appear, the penny dropped.

She slid open the side door, standing there in her dressing gown and rubbing her eyes. 'What is it? I was asleep.'

I stood to one side and pointed.

My goodness,' she exclaimed. 'What ever is it?'

I smiled and said it was our very own son et lumière display, minus the son!

Then I explained: standing on the outside table was her old china bowl she'd filled with water a while back. The sunlight at that time of morning was striking the surface of the water and projecting its image onto the wall. Swimming in the bowl was her collection of tadpoles that were busy growing from the handful of frog's eggs she'd scooped from the fish pond. The movement of the tadpoles as they swam their ever decreasing circles, before growing legs, was the cause of the constantly changing image.

'Oh, my God!' Dot exclaimed. 'Isn't that marvellous?'

I had to agree, but couldn't help adding the tadpole-driven display to the worm farm and wondering what her next little venture might be.